Alex and Roy:
Best Friends

Alex swung his arms around himself like a human helicopter. There was a loud crashing sound and a great stack of tapes fell to the floor.

"Idiot!" hissed Roy.

"What are you up to?" came Renee's voice.

Alex and Roy slid down into their beds and shut their eyes tight.

"I know you're not asleep," said Renee. "I heard you."

Alex and Roy tried to hold themselves perfectly still.

"Come on. What have you been up to?"

Alex wanted to giggle so much he began to shake.

Laugh with a Young Hippo Funny!

Bod's Mum's Knickers
Peter Beere

Emily H and the Enormous Tarantula
Kara May

Four Young Hippo Magic stories to enjoy:

My Friend's a Gris-Quok
Malorie Blackman

The Little Pet Dragon
Philippa Gregory

Broomstick Services
Ann Jungman

The Marmalade Pony
Linda Newbery

Ready for a Young Hippo Adventure?

Henry to the Rescue and Other Stories
Ruth Silvestre

Young Hippo Adventures for confident readers:

The Outfit Series –
The Secret of Weeping Wood
We Didn't Mean To, Honest!
Kidnap at Denton Farm
Robert Swindells

MARY DICKINSON

Alex and Roy:
Best Friends

Illustrated by Charlotte Firmin

Hippo

Scholastic Children's Books,
Scholastic Publications Ltd,
7–9 Pratt Street, London NW1 0AE, UK

Scholastic Inc.,
555 Broadway, New York, NY 10012-3999, USA

Scholastic Canada Ltd,
123 Newkirk Road, Richmond Hill,
Ontario, Canada L4C 3G5

Ashton Scholastic Pty Ltd,
P O Box 579, Gosford, New South Wales,
Australia

Ashton Scholastic Ltd,
Private Bag 94407, Greenmount, Auckland,
New Zealand

First published by André Deutsch Ltd, 1988
First published in paperback by Scholastic Publications Ltd, 1989
This edition by Scholastic Publications Ltd, 1995

ISBN 0 590 55943 5

Typeset by Contour Typesetters, Southall, London
Printed by Cox & Wyman Ltd, Reading, Berks

10 9 8 7 6 5 4 3 2 1

Contents

1 Roy's Cousins 7

2 The Dog 20

3 Trouble at the Café 31

4 A Trip Uptown 43

5 Playing Farms 55

6 Street Musicians 64

7 How Lucy Lost the Keys 77

8 The Airshow 91

9 The Night Out 103

10 Granny's Accident 117

11 The Patchwork Toboggan 130

12 The Robot 143

13 The Terrible Day 154

1
Roy's Cousins

It was midday and Alex was still in his pyjamas. His mother had been nagging him all morning to go and get dressed, but he kept on putting it off. Brring, brring! There was somebody at the door. Alex got dressed very quickly!

It was a good thing he did. Roy, his big sister Renee, and his little sister Bernice had come.

"We're going over to see our cousin Lizzie and her family," said Renee. "We wondered if Alex would like to come too. They've just moved into a new house that's got an enormous garden."

"What a good idea," said Alex's mother. "I need to do some shopping. That would be something for Alex to do, and someone for him to play with, instead of coming with me. What do you think, Alex?"

Alex didn't answer. He liked keeping his mother waiting.

Renee frowned. Alex was always very cheeky to his mother.

"Make up your mind. I can't wait all day," she snapped. "I'm sure you'll like it there. Lizzie's children, Paul and Karla, are about the same age as you."

"They've got hundreds of toys," added Roy.

"All right," said Alex slowly.

His mother sighed with relief. Quickly she found his coat and shoes. Gently, so he wouldn't notice, she dabbed at his hair with the hairbrush. He was ready! She bundled him towards the front door before he could change his mind.

Renee laughed at his sulky face. "Nobody'd ever guess that you and Roy are best friends."

They caught a bus on the main road. Alex and Roy sat in the front seats pretending to drive. There were shrieks from Bernice. She wanted to drive as well.

"You can't," said Roy. "You're too little."

"There's room for three on that seat," said Renee.

"There isn't!" replied Roy.

"Here's a little space," said Alex, squashing up against the window. He couldn't understand why Roy always wanted to leave Bernice out of their games. He would have liked a little brother or sister.

Bernice squeezed in between Alex and Roy.

"There's no room now," moaned Roy. "She always ruins things!"

They got off the bus outside a shop that sold flowers.

"I'll buy some for Lizzie," said Renee. "They'll cheer her up. She's been feeling a bit lonely and left out since they moved. She doesn't know anybody round here yet."

"Poor Lizzie," agreed Alex, little realizing it would soon be his turn to be left out.

It was only a short walk to Lizzie's house. Alex thought it looked like a proper "country" house, surrounded by trees, with a stone path wiggling across an enormous green lawn to the front door.

Lizzie came rushing out to meet them.

"Hi! It's good to see you. Come in, come in."

Alex felt a little unsure. Roy tugged at his arm. "Don't be shy. They're really nice."

But when they got inside the house Roy was whisked away from Alex by Lizzie. She wanted to see how big he'd grown. Bernice and Renee talked to Steve, Lizzie's husband. Paul and Karla bounced excitedly around them. And nobody took any notice of Alex. He stood alone and watched them all, feeling left out. A large wolf-like dog padded into the room and looked around. It noticed Alex, walked straight up to him, sniffed his legs and sat down next to him. Then, looking up at Alex, it opened its mouth to reveal two long rows of big white teeth.

Help! thought Alex. He was frightened of dogs. He raised his arms in the air, hopefully out of its reach.

Then Roy came over, but he didn't seem to notice Alex. He put his arms around the dog's neck.

"Hello, Major. How are you?" he asked. "Do you like your new home?"

I don't like it here, thought Alex. I wish I'd never come.

"We're going to play upstairs," shouted Paul and Karla. "Coming, Alex and Roy?"

Roy stood up and bounded up the stairs after them, Major trotted off somewhere, and Alex found himself alone once more. He felt cross. Nobody had waited for him.

"Why aren't you playing with the other children?" asked Lizzie.

Alex shook his head. "They don't want me."

"Rubbish!" said Lizzie. "But you can stay here if you like. You could read these." She handed Alex a pile of comics.

He flipped through them, but he didn't feel much like reading. He could hear the other children bumping and laughing away upstairs.

"Cheer up, Alex," said Steve kindly. "Come and give me a hand in the garden. I've an old car tyre and some rope. I'm going to try and make a swing."

"All right," mumbled Alex, shrugging his shoulders as if he didn't care. He did really. He liked Steve being his friend.

The garden at the back of the house was even bigger than the front. Right at the bottom there were three tall trees.

Steve pointed up at a branch. "I've got to get the rope over there. It would be easy if I had a ladder. But I haven't. We're going to have to throw it over."

He had a go. Alex had a go. They kept on just missing. It was infuriating, but it did make Alex forget to feel sad.

At last Steve threw the rope over. He and Alex jumped in the air to celebrate, then he tied the rope around the tyre. "Be the first on the new swing, Alex," he commanded.

Alex clambered up and sat in the tyre. Steve held it still while he climbed, but once Alex was on he twisted it round and round. Then he let go. Alex went spinning. Everything swayed. He was dizzy.

"Do it again! Again!" cried Alex.

Roy saw him from an upstairs window and dashed down.

"Budge up," he said, hauling himself up.

Paul looked out of the window. They waved and shouted for him to join them.

He hurried over, and struggled on to the tyre. There was only just room.

Then Karla saw them.

"Oh, no!" groaned Paul. "There's not enough room."

Karla came running. She didn't slow down. She threw herself up, on top of the boys. There were awful screams and howls. "Ouch! My finger! My leg! Karla, get off my leg! Oooh, you scratched me. Get off! I can't breathe. You're squashing me. Karla, get off!"

But Karla clutched tightly to the rope and refused to move. She enjoyed annoying the boys.

Bernice wandered out. She looked curiously at the bundle of screeching, swinging children. She was too small to climb up by herself, so she raised her arms in the air ready to be picked up, and screamed.

"What a noise!" winced Paul. "Let's climb up to the branch; the babies won't get us up there."

So the boys scrambled up the rope. Karla

tried to follow, but couldn't reach. "Stupid boys," she said, sticking out her tongue. "I didn't want to play with you, anyway."

She jumped down from the tyre and marched back towards the house looking stiff and cross.

"I don't know," moaned Steve. "There's always somebody left out."

He picked up Bernice and jogged after Karla. Bernice giggled at every step. "Wait, Karla!" he called. "It's nearly suppertime. You can help me get it ready."

The boys tumbled down from the tree. "Did you say supper?"

"Only if you help," said Steve.

Never had the kitchen been so busy. Roy and Alex got the job of doing the sandwiches. Alex kept making holes in his slices of bread. He stuck his finger through one and made Roy laugh. Karla laid the table because she knew where to find all the things. Bernice put cakes from a packet out on a plate. She picked at the chocolate bits, but everybody was too busy to notice. Paul somehow managed to do nothing.

Just before supper was ready, Steve gave Paul some money, and all the children walked down to the shop to choose themselves a can of drink. Alex felt very happy. He held Bernice's hand and helped her to keep up with the rest.

Steve watched them go. He smiled to himself. "Everyone happy. I wonder how long that will last?"

It lasted all evening.

After supper they played a card game. An easy one so Bernice could join in. Suddenly Renee realized it was very late.

"Alex and Roy could stay the night if they liked," said Lizzie. "We could phone your mother, Alex, and ask if that'd be all right."

Alex thought a moment. It was good being

with lots of people, but back at his home his mother would fuss over him. She would tuck him up in bed, hug him and tell him all about her day. She might even have bought him something when she was out shopping.

"Thanks," said Alex, "but I'd rather go home."

2
The Dog

Not long after the visit to his cousins, Roy started spending a lot of time watching dogs, and talking about dogs.

"I wish I had a dog," he told Alex one day. "I wonder if Mum would let me have one? We haven't got a pet."

Alex shuddered deep down at the thought of Roy having a dog. He was afraid of dogs. They could growl, bite, slap you with their tails. Knock you over.

Roy soon noticed how scared he was, and how easy it was to tease him.

"There's a lovely big black dog in the playground today," grinned Roy. "Come and see."

"Don't want to," sniffed Alex.

"Renee's friend's got a Tiger dog. It escaped last night. She says it's here somewhere."

Alex knew, or almost knew, Roy was only teasing. But he didn't want to risk it. "I've got to go home now," he said.

After a while he got so fed up with Roy and his dogs he refused even to go out and play.

"Coming out?" called Roy.

"Too busy," replied Alex.

Alex's mother thought it a shame they weren't friends any more. "Why don't you phone Roy? Invite him over."

Alex shook his head firmly.

She began to get cross with him. He was always in her way.

"I must tidy up," she said. "This whole flat is like a dump. Will you go and play outside, please!"

"I want to play inside," said Alex stubbornly, pulling out his car box.

"I'll sweep you up," threatened his mother.

Alex pretended not to hear. He took a car from the box.

"I'll tidy you on to the top shelf," she threatened again.

Alex took another car from the box.

"Right!" said his mother, who was furious by now. "I'm going to throw you and your cars into the bin." She picked him up, carried him out of his bedroom, through the hall, opened the front door, held him over the bin for a moment, then dumped him on the

doorstep. She went inside, shutting the door sharply behind her.

"Mum! I don't want to play outside," shouted Alex. He pressed the doorbell for as long as his finger could press. The birds heard and flew away. The cats heard and looked surprised, but somehow his mother just didn't hear.

"Hey, Alex! What you doing?" called a voice from below.

Alex looked over the balcony wall. It was Roy on his bike.

"Coming out on your bike?" he enquired.

Alex took a quick look around. There were no dogs about.

"Yes," he shouted. "If I can get it. Mum's cleaning and won't let me in."

"I'll come up," called Roy. "Give you a hand."

They took it in turns to ring the doorbell. When at last Alex's mother answered she was very, very angry. "What do you want?"

"Can I get my bike out, please?" asked Alex.

Alex's mother gave a big sigh. Then she noticed Roy and smiled with relief. They were friends again! "I should have known you'd change your mind. Wait a minute. I'll get your bike."

She was soon back. "Remember," she warned. "Ride on the path and not on the road."

"Yes, Mum," promised Alex.

Alex and Roy rode round the flats. It was a warm day, lots of children were out playing, but there were no dogs. Then, suddenly, coming round a sharp corner, Alex did meet a dog.

"Woof!" said the dog in surprise.

"Oh!" said Alex in surprise, and he and his bike toppled over with a crash.

Alex lay on the path, his bike on top of him. His knee hurt. There was blood trickling down his leg. He wanted his mum, but there was nobody about but the dog. To his horror it walked towards him, right up to him, and licked his face!

Alex was terrified. "Go away, horrible dog," he cried. "It's all your fault."

"What's up?" asked Roy, pedalling round the corner. "That dog won't hurt you. It's a nice dog. I've seen it before."

"I've hurt my knee," sniffed Alex. "It's bleeding."

"I'll take you home," said Roy.

He helped Alex free himself from the bike and, with arms round each other, they stumbled back to Alex's flat. They had to ring the doorbell a long time before Alex's mother would answer.

"Not back already," she began. Then she noticed Alex's knee. "Oh, dear. How did you do that? It looks very painful. Come into the kitchen and I'll clean it up."

Alex sat on the kitchen table while his mother gently washed his knee. Roy watched. Alex told her about the horrible, horrible dog that had come round the corner and knocked him off his bike.

"Poor Alex," said his mother. "Never mind. We'll cover your knee with a plaster; have a slice of chocolate cake, and you'll soon feel better."

Alex's mother had just cut one slice when she stopped. "By the way, where's your bike now, Alex?"

"Don't know," said Alex. "Where I fell off, I suppose."

"Oh, Alex," cried his mother. "You are silly. Someone might take it."

Roy suddenly looked frightened. "I left my bike there, too. I had to help Alex."

"We must go and get them now," said Alex's mother. She unhooked her keys and made for the door. Alex snatched the piece of cake and followed her with Roy.

Outside, the dustcart had arrived. It was being loaded with rubbish. Alex had a quick look to check that nobody had thrown away his bike. It was all right, no bike inside.

They walked round Alex's flats on to the main road. A group of girls came cycling past. Alex stared hard at their bikes to check his wasn't there. No. They were all girls' bikes.

Round the back by the garages, two women were loading something into a car boot. It was the same colour as Alex's bike. He ran to get a closer look. It was a lawn mower!

Then they came to a corner that you couldn't see round. "This is it," shouted Alex. And sure enough there was Alex's bike, and Roy's bike, and the dog. It seemed to be guarding the bikes.

Alex's mother sighed with relief. "Seems as if it wasn't such a horrible dog after all. It was looking after your bikes till you came back."

Alex was happy. "Thank you, dog," he said, very carefully patting its head. The dog wagged its tail and, with one whisk of its tongue, gobbled up the rather squashed piece of chocolate cake that Alex was still holding in his hand.

"Hey, that's my cake," cried Alex, but he didn't mind too much. He was feeling better already. His mother said he could have another piece when they got home.

Alex wiped his sticky hand on his trousers, picked up his bike and, before Roy had even got to his bike, pedalled off shouting, "Beat you back!"

But Alex didn't win the race. The dog did. It bounded alongside Alex, sort of sideways, so it could look at him all the time. It arrived panting, first, at Alex's steps. When his mother and Roy arrived Alex was hugging the dog, thanking him for looking after his bike.

"Funny how things turn out," laughed Alex's mother. "Today started out such a terrible day. But here we are, you boys friends again, Alex no longer frightened of dogs, *and* I managed to tidy Alex's room!"

3

Trouble at the Café

It was one of those days when there seemed to be nothing to do at Alex's house. There were jobs like helping with the washing up, tidying his bedroom and sweeping the hall, but Alex didn't fancy these. He decided to go and visit Roy. See what he was doing.

Alex liked visiting Roy. His house was such a busy place. There was always someone to talk to or something going on. Best of all Alex liked their living room with its two settees, both very bouncy. You could bounce right up into the air. Roy's mother would shriek if she caught anyone doing it.

It was she who opened the door to Alex.

"Oh, come in," she exclaimed. "Roy will be pleased to see you. Renee and Bernice have gone out shopping. It's very quiet in here."

Roy was sitting on one of the settees, drawing. He didn't see Alex enter the room. He was feeling a little cross. He'd just asked his mother if he could have a dog and she'd said no.

I'll surprise him, thought Alex. Have a bounce as well. He sprang on to the settee next to Roy. "Hello!"

"Oh, Alex!" screamed Roy, furious. "You've ruined my drawing. Go away."

He gave Alex a push. Alex pushed back. Soon there was a tangle of arms and legs and shouts. A full-scale fight was on.

"Stop that!" shouted Roy's mother. "I thought you two were friends. Haven't you got anything better to do?"

"If I had a dog I could take it for a walk," said Roy stubbornly. "But you won't let me have one."

Roy's mother shook her head. "If you had a dog it would be me who looked after it. Me who fed it. Me who paid for it."

"I would look after it," argued Roy. "And I'll pay for it."

"You've no money," reminded his mother.

"I'll save up," said Roy.

His mother laughed.

Roy felt determined. He marched towards the door. "I'll get a job. That's what I'll do. Come on, Alex, let's see what we can find."

Roy's mother smiled. She didn't hold out much hope of them getting a job. But at least they weren't fighting.

She was right. Nobody wanted their path swept, their car washed, their dog walked. When they offered to help an old lady she waved her umbrella at them, said they were trying to rob her and threatened to call the police. Disheartened, they wandered back to Roy's house hoping there was something good on TV.

"Could you do a job for me?" called a voice when they were nearly back. Their big chance? No; just the postman with a parcel for Roy's mother. "Take this in, please," he said.

"I wonder what's in it?" puzzled Alex. "It's heavy and hard and rectangular shaped."

They couldn't guess, but Roy's mother knew the moment she saw it. "That's my new toaster. I ordered it from the catalogue. I got café size. You can cook six pieces at once."

"Café!" grinned Roy. "We could have a café. We'd soon have lots of money."

"And where are you going to have this café?" enquired Roy's mother.

"In the kitchen," said Roy.

His mother shook her head. "Oh, no, you're not."

"Please, Mum. Just today," pleaded Roy. "Alex and I will do all the work. Honest we will. Honest."

Roy's mother thought a moment. "Okay.

Only today, and you'd better not make any mess."

The first thing they did was write the menu: all the things you could have with toast. Beans on toast. Spaghetti on toast. Honey on toast. Butter on toast. Soup with toast. They soon realized they needed to buy some food. They persuaded Roy's mother to take them shopping.

"I must be crazy," she sighed. "It would be easier and cheaper just to say yes to a dog."

To make her feel happier Alex and Roy took it in turns to wheel the shopping basket for her.

They felt very excited as they paid for their goods and loaded them into the basket. They told the man at the checkout all about their café.

Back home they tidied up the kitchen. Cleared, cleaned and laid the table. Alex neatly arranged their food near the toaster.

Roy made a sign that said "OPEN", and hung it on the front door.

Hardly a minute had passed before in strolled Fat Bob. He lived in the next block. The man at the checkout had told him about the new café.

"Felt a bit hungry. Thought I'd pop in for a snack," he said.

Alex showed him the menu.

"I'll have soup and toast to start," said Fat Bob. "Followed by beans on toast, and then a piece of toast and honey."

Alex and Roy got busy. Roy put the bread in the toaster, while Alex opened the tins and tipped them into saucepans. Roy's mother heated them up for him. When it was ready Alex and Roy carried it over to Fat Bob on trays.

"Looks good," he said, and started eating.

Alex and Roy watched Fat Bob. He seemed to enjoy his snack. He ate it all. They weren't sure what to do when he'd finished.

"The bill," whispered Roy's mother. "Add up what he's had and give him the bill."

She helped them with the prices, but made them do the adding up themselves. She said it was good practice. It was quite a while before they got the answer right! Roy took it over to Fat Bob on a plate.

"Oh, no," he gasped. "He's asleep."

"Make a noise. Tell him his bill's come," suggested Roy's mother.

"Your bill!" said Roy, banging the plate down on the table.

Fat Bob gave a start, but went on sleeping. The café owners looked sadly at one another. "Better wash up," said Roy's mother.

They washed up. They swept up. But still Fat Bob slept. Then they heard some-one come in the front door. It was Renee and Bernice returning from their shopping trip.

"Hello, everybody," yawned Renee, flopping into an armchair. "I've had a dreadful day. Bernice has driven me up the wall. She won't do this and she won't do that. She goes on all the time wanting sweets and ice-cream and Coke. On and on and on. Worst of all she's got a new trick of pinching people. She pinched the girl in front of us on the bus. Made her scream . . ."

At that moment there was an "Aaaaah!" from Fat Bob.

"Oh, no," said Renee. "She's done it again. Why's he here, anyway?"

Roy's mother explained, while Alex and Roy rushed over to Fat Bob with the bill.

Fat Bob rubbed his eyes sleepily. "Sorry. I'm always doing that. Something about

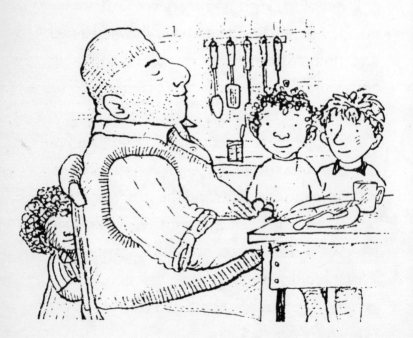

eating always sends me to sleep. Here's a little extra money for any inconvenience." He heaved himself to his feet and plodded out of the door.

Alex and Roy shared the money between them.

"I'm hot," said Alex. "I'm going to buy an ice-cream."

"So am I," agreed Roy.

"Thought the money was for your dog?" reminded his mother.

Poor Roy; he did so feel like an ice-cream.

"Come here," ordered Renee. She put some money in his hand. "If you take Bernice with you and buy her an ice-cream, you can keep the change for your dog. But walk slowly. I don't want to see her again for at least half an hour."

So Alex and Roy and Bernice wandered down to the shop.

Alex couldn't quite understand how little Bernice could hurt anybody. But he kindly held her hand tightly on his side, just in case.

4
A Trip Uptown

As a very special, extra exciting, extremely expensive treat, Alex's mother took Alex and Roy uptown to look round a museum. She decided to pop in and see her old friend Sylvie while they were there.

They went by train. It was very exciting. Through the windows they saw many things: tractors, cows, chimneys, cranes, boats, a motorway with tiny cars on it. The train went faster than the cars.

When they arrived even the station was exciting. There were shops and stalls. Alex wanted everything. "Can I have a big balloon? Can I have a furry monkey? I'm hungry. Can we have a beefburger? Can we go in a taxi?"

"I wish I could buy you all you wanted," said his mother. "But I haven't the money."

"Would this help?" said Roy, pulling a coin from his pocket. "It's really for the dog I'm going to get, but you can have it if you like."

Alex's mother gave him a little hug. "Thank you, Roy, but you keep it. It's your savings."

They went down an escalator and along a tunnel to catch an underground train. It was exciting and frightening all in one.

They heard music echoing through the tunnel. As they walked it got louder. It was getting nearer. They saw a woman with a guitar and a man with a drum, standing, playing, at the side of the tunnel. Alex and Roy stopped to watch.

"They're good, aren't they?" said Roy.

The woman's guitar case lay open by her side. People threw money in as they passed.

"I'm going to throw my money in," said Roy. And he did.

"Come on," shouted Alex's mother. "We haven't got all day."

The museum was not very exciting. There were animals in glass cases, stuffed and not alive. There were old cars and small aeroplanes, but you weren't allowed to touch. There were tables with specimens on, too high up for the boys to see. They were glad when Alex's mother said it was time to go to Sylvie's.

They caught a double-decker bus, which luckily was full downstairs, so they had to go up. They grabbed seats by the windows so they could have a good look out. It was a bit like being a giant. They could see in upstairs windows, and look down on the tops of cars. They were almost as high as the chimneys! Unfortunately they soon had to get off.

Sylvie's house was right next to the bus stop. It was a very big house, with wide grey steps, and tall white pillars each side of an enormous front door.

"Phew!" said Roy. "Does your friend live here?"

Alex's mother nodded.

They pressed a bell. A crackly voice spoke from a box near the door. "Hello . . . Good . . . Come in."

The door sprang open as if by magic. They stepped into a large hall. There was a wide staircase and lots of doors. A woman came out of one. She wore a matching skirt and jacket. She looked like somebody out of a magazine. It was Sylvie.

She gave a big hug to Alex's mother, and smiled at Alex and Roy. "Hello. Glad you could come. You must be worn out tramping round that museum."

They followed her into a very big room.

"Sit down," she continued. "I'll make some tea."

Alex stared around the room. At first he thought it must be Sylvie's bedroom because there was a neatly made up bed. But then he saw a stove, and a sink, and a fridge. By the window were a table and chairs. A whole flat in one room? He pointed the things out to Roy.

"But where's the bathroom?" wondered Roy.

They looked around. There were two doors in the room.

"Which one?" puzzled Alex.

"We came in that one, silly!" said Roy, pointing to the larger door. "So it must be the other one."

Without thinking to ask they dashed across the room and opened the door. It wasn't the bathroom. It was a cupboard, with shelves heaped full of strangely shaped objects. It was hard to tell what was there, the cupboard was so dark. It looked very interesting. Alex was ready to investigate when Sylvie said, "Are you looking for the bathroom?"

"Er, yes," mumbled Alex and Roy.

"It's through the other door. First door on the left. I'll show you."

She led them out into the hall, and opened a door.

"Here it is. There's a toilet as well. You could wash your hands before eating tea. Okay?" She left them there.

The funny thing was, Alex and Roy didn't

want to go to the bathroom. They only wanted to know where it was. When Sylvie had gone they laughed and laughed. They inspected the toilet and checked that it flushed. They tried the taps in the sink and smelt the soap . . . pooh! They tried the taps in the bath too, and the shower. They nearly got soaked.

"Let's explore upstairs," said Alex.

They climbed the stairs slowly and quietly. There were more doors and more stairs. Suddenly a man came out of a door.

"What are you boys doing here?" he asked crossly.

"Mum's with Sylvie," gulped Alex.

The man nodded sternly and went back inside.

"Let's go down," said Alex. He felt uneasy. "I want to see what's in that cupboard."

Sylvie welcomed them back. Tea was ready.

When they'd eaten, Alex asked in his politest way, "Could we look at the things in your cupboard, please?"

"Of course," said Sylvie. "There's a light switch just inside the door."

The cupboard was full of strange things. Creamy shells, wooden baskets. Large round mats, pots with criss-cross patterns. Pipes with bulges; drums covered in real furs tied around with strings. Scary deep brown statues with wicked picked out eyes. More and more and more things. Alex and Roy were amazed.

"Can we touch them?" Alex asked.

"If you're careful."

"What's this?" asked Roy.

Sylvie explained. She knew about all the things. She'd collected them on her travels. There was a story to go with everything.

"I spend all my money on travelling," she

51

said. "It's what I enjoy. That's why I live in just one room."

Alex thought Sylvie was wonderful, much better than the museum.

Alex's mother was a little fed up. She'd been looking forward to a good old gossip, and Sylvie was spending all her time talking to Alex and Roy.

At home time Alex's mother insisted they put all the things carefully back in the cupboard. Alex secretly hoped Sylvie might give him one of the drums, or even a rock from the rock collection. He kept saying how much he liked them, but Sylvie only smiled and said, "I'm glad you enjoyed my collection." However, when they left she gave Alex and Roy a little money each, for their savings.

They caught the bus again. It was no fun this time, everybody was going home. There were no seats, they had to stand. They couldn't even see out of the windows.

At the underground station they joined a stampede of people. It swept them down the steps, down the escalator, and along a tunnel towards the trains. They heard the music again. Not the same as before. This time there was only one musician. A man with a big golden saxophone. Alex wanted to stop, but his mother pushed him on.

"I want to get home," she snapped.

Alex wanted to stay. He remembered what Roy had done to the first musicians. He tossed a coin into the man's money hat. Chink. Alex noticed there was quite a lot of money in the hat. It looked as if being a musician was a good way to earn money. He began to wonder . . .

There was a sharp pain on his arm and he was nearly tugged off his feet. He'd been grabbed by his mother.

"If you don't come along, this'll be the last treat you ever get!"

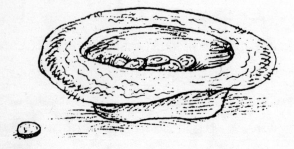

5
Playing Farms

Alex and Roy's trip uptown gave them much to think about. They found the musicians in the Underground especially interesting. Alex felt sure that to be a musician was a good way to earn a fortune. It would be easy. They needn't go uptown, they could play somewhere near his home. He had a hat he could use to collect the money in. All he needed to do was find a musical instrument to play. He asked his mother to help him.

After some moments of thought she said that "somewhere" she had a recorder. It was a kind of wooden whistle that she'd had when she was at school. The problem was, where was that "somewhere"?

"Please find it," nagged Alex. "Please, please. I need it right now."

"It'll have to be later," said Alex's mother. "Granny's coming and I must tidy up."

"Please, please," Alex wailed on. He followed his mother from room to room, standing close to her elbow. He knew it annoyed her. She would soon give in.

"Oh, all right," she said at last. "I think it must be under the stairs. That's where I keep all my old junk."

She opened the door of the understairs cupboard and immediately a box of toys fell out and tumbled over the floor.

"That's where my transporter went," said

Alex angrily. He got down on his knees and looked at the toys in the box. "And my tanker, and my. . ."

"Alex!" screamed his mother. "Put those toys back in the box. You can play with them later. We're looking for a recorder, remember?"

Alex nodded and lazily threw the toys back into the box. His mother was groaning, "Ooh . . . Aah . . . Oooh." She was grappling with a large object in the cupboard. At last she heaved out a TV.

"Another TV!" said Alex. "Can I have it?"

"No," said his mother. "It doesn't work. I'm going to get it fixed one day."

"Please," said Alex.

"No," said his mother. She dived back into the cupboard and pulled out a tall lamp with a very long lead. She had to pull and pull to get it all out.

"I need a lamp," said Alex. "Can I have that one?"

"No," said his mother. "There's something wrong with it. It keeps on falling over."

"Please," said Alex.

"No," said his mother.

Next she pulled out an old lawnmower.

"No," she said before Alex could even ask.

After that came a cardboard box tied up with string.

"Can I have it?" Alex asked quickly.

"I can't remember what it is," puzzled Alex's mother. She smiled at Alex. "We'd better open it and see, hadn't we?"

She undid the string and pulled up the flaps. She gasped with surprise. "It's my old farm set. I used to play with it when I was your age, Alex. It's ever so good. There's cows and sheep, and horses and pigs and chickens and ducks."

She took them out of the box and stood

them up. One cow had a matchstick for a leg and had to lean against the box.

"There's stables too, and a pig sty, and trees and fences, and a chicken coop, and a farm house," went on Alex's mother.

"Here's the farmer's wife. She's always busy feeding the chickens. And here's Mr Field. He drives the red tractor all over the

place." Alex's mother made a berrrrrrering noise. It made her lips wobble. She pushed the tractor round and round. "And here's the red and brown trailer that hooks on behind the tractor."

Alex was silent. He thought the farm set was wonderful.

His mother got some more things out of the box. "This lorry here belongs to bad Mr Grimey, the scrap metal dealer." She drove it along the carpet with a deep ummmmmming sound. "He drives up and takes Farmer Field's old fences and ploughs away," she explained and piled some toys into the back of the lorry and drove off again.

"Mr Grimey drives home," continued Alex's mother. "But oh, dear! Farmer Field notices Mr Grimey has taken his new plough and not his old one. He got it wrong! So . . . Farmer Field jumps into his sports car and chases Mr Grimey. Meeeeowerrrrrr."

Alex's mother pushed the cars until she was almost lying on her tummy. And at that moment the front door opened and in came Alex's granny. "Hello, you two. It's only me. The door was open so I let myself in. Are you busy?"

She saw the farm all over the floor and thought at once that it was Alex who was playing. "Oh, Alex. What a mess," she said. "Don't you ever put your toys away? Why do you have to play here in the hall? It makes such a mess for your poor mother to clear up."

"It's not me," said Alex indignantly. "It's Mummy. She's having a tidy-up."

"Tidying up!" said Granny in amazement. Then she saw the farm set. "Oh," she groaned. "I remember that farm set. I broke a cow's leg once, tripping over it. Your mother never used to put it away."

"I got it out for Alex," explained his

mother. "We were really looking for my old recorder. I thought it was in this cupboard."

"Come with me, Alex," said Granny in her "no nonsense" voice. "Your mum's busy and I've got something for you." And arm in arm like naughty friends they swept into the kitchen leaving Alex's mother grumbling and tidying up.

Granny scrabbled in her carrier bag and brought out a little red trumpet with a silky tassel. It was for Alex.

It was just what he wanted. He was overjoyed. "Thank you, Granny, thank you," he said.

He went and showed his mother. She didn't seem very pleased. She even seemed a bit cross. "It's lovely," she said quickly. Alex couldn't make out what he'd done wrong.

Later he found out. It wasn't him she was cross with, it was Granny! She told Granny off!

"I wish you'd told me you were going to buy Alex a musical instrument," snapped Alex's mother, "then I wouldn't have had to turn the cupboard out. It's taken me all morning!"

6

Street Musicians

Alex was very proud of the trumpet his granny gave him. It was red, made of plastic, with a floppy gold tassel swinging from a gold cord. It wasn't as big as a real trumpet and didn't sound much like a real trumpet, but Alex loved it. He tooted and tooted all day. Granny began to wonder if perhaps it had been a mistake to give Alex such a noisy present.

"Can't you toot it outside?" she suggested. "I thought you and Roy were going to be street musicians and earn yourselves a fortune?"

"Oh, yes," said Alex. "I nearly forgot. I'll go round to Roy's; see if he's got anything to play."

He went and found his summer straw hat and put it on. They could use it to collect the money in.

Alex's mother and Granny wished him well. "Be back in time for dinner," they called after him.

Bernice opened the door to Alex. "Shhh," she said loudly, finger to her lips. "We're playing quietly. Mum's got a bad head."

Roy was pleased to see Alex. He was meant to be in charge of Bernice. She was being noisy and not doing a thing he asked.

He looked puzzledly at Alex. "What you

got that silly hat on for?"

"It's my money collecting hat," explained Alex. "I thought we could be musicians like we saw uptown."

He showed Roy his new trumpet.

"That's good," said Roy. "Let's have a go."

Alex handed him the trumpet.

Toot te toot toot, toot te tooo, played Roy.

"I wanna go," cried Bernice.

"No," said Roy.

"I don't mind," said Alex.

So Bernice blew, teeeoot, teeoot, teeeoot!

"Shh," said Roy. "You'll wake Mum."

"Have you got anything to play?" asked Alex.

Roy looked around. He noticed a round picture of a beach and palm trees on the bookcase. He got it down and showed Alex. It was really a tambourine. When he thumped it against his leg, silvery discs set into the side made shuddery ringing sounds. When he tapped the picture, it sounded like a drum.

"That's great," said Alex. "We've got a band. Are you coming out?"

"We'd better practise," said Roy. "All musicians practise."

"Okay," said Alex, and he put his hat down on the carpet.

Toot te toot. Tash, tttash, tashh. Toot, tooot tooo.

"I wanna go," said Bernice, reaching out.

"No," said Roy. "This is our band." He went on playing.

Bernice was not going to be left out. She made more grabs at Roy's tambourine. He held it above his head so she couldn't reach.

Bernice wasn't easily beaten. She clambered on to the back of the settee to make herself taller. When that didn't work she jumped up and down screaming. Finally, with a desperate look on her face, she picked up Alex's hat and put it on her head.

"Give that back," shouted Roy.

"No," said Bernice.

Roy grabbed the rim of the hat. Bernice held it tightly to her head. A tug of war followed.

"Stop!" shouted Alex. "You'll tear it."

There was a sudden bang. The living room door had been flung open. Roy's mother stood in the doorway looking tired-eyed and furious.

"What is going on?" she yelled. "I can't rest with all this noise."

Roy explained about Alex's idea, how they were practising, and how Bernice was trying to grab his tambourine.

"What a good idea, Alex," said Roy's mother. "If you all went out it would be good and quiet in this house. Let me think if there's anything Bernice could play. I know. There's an old guitar in the toy cupboard. Most of the strings are broken, but it'll do for Bernice."

"She's too little to play," complained Roy.

"I wanna play," repeated Bernice, wiggling the brim of Alex's hat up and down.

Alex was sure she would break his hat doing that. He went to the toy cupboard, found the guitar and gave it to Bernice. She gave him back his hat.

"Good, you're ready now," said Roy's mother. She opened the front door and pointed for them to leave. Alex and Roy led the way, and Bernice followed twanging the guitar.

When Alex thought they were at a good spot, on the path that led to the shops, he put his hat on the ground and raised his trumpet to his lips.

"Ready, everybody?"

"*You* are not to play," Roy told Bernice.

"One, two, three!" called Alex.

Toot toot toot. Tap rattle, tap rrrattle.

Twang, twang. Bernice was joining in.

"You're not to play," hissed Roy.

Bernice smiled in a teasing sort of way, and went on playing.

Roy gave up. There was nothing he could do but bang his tambourine louder and louder.

The path was a busy place. Lots of people walked by, but nobody stopped to listen or throw money into Alex's hat. In fact they seemed to walk faster when they passed by. The only person to stop was a girl from Alex and Roy's school, Wendy.

"What are you doing?" she asked. "Can I join in?"

They stopped playing.

Roy nodded. "You can use the guitar. Bernice isn't playing."

But Bernice wanted to play. When Wendy tried to take the guitar from her she wouldn't let go. She wrapped her arms tightly around it and screamed, "Mine!" There was a struggle and the one working string broke. Bernice wailed as if heartbroken.

"What can I play now?" demanded Wendy.

Alex shrugged his shoulders in an unhelpful way. He hadn't really wanted Wendy in their band in the first place, and now she'd broken the guitar and made Bernice cry. He felt a little sorry for Bernice.

"There's a lot of people coming," shouted Roy.

They started playing again, as loud as they could to drown the sound of Bernice's crying. Suddenly Wendy began to dance! Alex wrinkled up his nose in disgust. Whoever heard of dancing street musicians! Roy looked the other way, it was too awful. But then there was a chinking noise, a passer-by had thrown some money into Alex's hat. A few minutes later somebody else did too.

Alex and Roy looked painfully at each
other; Wendy had her hands above her head
now. She was clapping and wriggling her
middle, a bit like the beaters in an electric
mixer. Bernice was copying her.

But . . . Chink . . . Chink. More money in
the hat.

Next Wendy started to sing. "Ooh ah wa
wa waa. Oooh ah wa wa waa." Alex cringed.

Chink. Chink. More money going into the
hat.

Poor Alex and Roy, they were torn between the nice sound of chinking money, and the terrible sound of Wendy singing. Should they go on playing or give up?

Wendy's mother decided it. "Wendee!" she called. "Wendee! Your dinner's ready."

Wendy stopped. "I've got to go. How much money have we got?"

Roy tipped the money out on to the path. It looked a lot, but they were all small coins. Wendy counted them.

"Fifteen," she said. "That's good, we can divide it into three. I get five, Alex gets five, Roy gets five. That's fair, isn't it?"

She scooped up her five and ran off. "See you after dinner," she shouted back.

Alex shook his head. "I'm not coming back after dinner. It's not worth it. This much money after all that playing."

He put the money into his pocket and his hat back on his head.

"We'll have to think up another way to earn money," he said. "Any ideas?"

Roy had none.

"Might as well go home, then," said Alex. "It must be my dinner time too. Where's my trumpet?"

Bernice had it, and the tambourine. She grinned and started to play them both at once.

Teeeeoot, bang. Teeeoot, bang.

Alex and Roy sighed. They didn't have the energy to fight her any more. Roy screwed up his face and covered his ears. "What a noise!"

"Let's go home quick," said Alex.

They walked back as fast as they could, trying to leave Bernice and her noise as far behind them as possible. They had to let her catch them up when it was time to cross the road.

When they got back to Roy's they realized

that Bernice had left the guitar behind on the path.

Roy had to run all the way back to get it!

"Now do you understand about little sisters?" he said to Alex when he returned.

7

How Lucy Lost the Keys

The sun beat down outside Alex's flats. The heat made the concrete seem to shiver. It was too hot for bike riding. Alex and Roy leaned on their handlebars, not knowing what to do, feeling like doing nothing. Somewhere in the flats a baby was crying. It went on crying and crying.

"Why don't you boys come and have a

drink?" called down Alex's mother. So they went in.

All the windows of Alex's flat were open. Even inside you could hear the baby crying.

"Poor thing," said Alex's mother. "It must be hot."

They heard someone scream at the baby.

"That's Sue's voice," said Alex's mother. "The heat's getting to her too. Mind you, I feel a bit hot and restless myself. You'd better be good or I'll be screaming at you!"

"We've got nothing to do," moaned Alex.

"Well," began his mother, taking a deep breath and resting her chin in her hand.

Alex and Roy waited.

"What about a trip to the seaside?" she asked at last. "Perhaps your mum and Bernice would like to come, Roy? There's plenty of room in the car."

Roy pulled a face of terror. "Not Bernice. She spoils everything."

"But I need a friend," explained Alex's mother. "I'll ask Sue and little Lucy. Lucy would love the sand."

Alex and Roy groaned. Perhaps Bernice would have been better than a baby.

Alex's mother was pleased with her plan. "It's always good to help someone out," she said.

Sue thought it a lovely idea; but she wondered if they could take Lucy on her own. There were a lot of things she needed to do at home.

Alex's mother said, "That's all right." Though it meant she still didn't have a friend for herself.

Then Alex remembered Granny. He phoned and asked her to come.

"I'll be over in half an hour," said Granny.

In the next half-hour everyone was very busy.

Roy rushed home to ask if he could go.

Alex's mother made up a picnic, found the swimming things, and fitted Alex's old baby seat into the car for Lucy. Alex made a collection of toys to play in the sand with.

"Are you sure you'll need all those?" laughed his mother when she saw the large bag.

Granny arrived with another large bag, and another picnic box.

Goody, thought Alex: two picnics!

Roy returned carrying his swimming things and a large bottle of orange drink. Lucy and her mother arrived with another large bag.

"I hope we're all going to fit in," worried Alex's mother.

It was a bit of a squash. Alex and Roy moaned about the baby seat taking up all the room, but it did keep Lucy safely strapped in one place. She cried terribly when they all waved goodbye to Sue and drove off, but two minutes later she was fast asleep. Granny had a packet of ginger snaps in her bag. She offered them to Alex and Roy whenever they began to complain.

"They'll never eat their dinner," moaned Alex's mother.

There was great excitement when the car finally stopped at the top of a long sandy beach. Granny seemed to be the most excited of all. She was first out of the car and off over the sand to find a good spot. Alex's mother was left to unload the car.

"It's going to take several journeys, all this stuff," she sighed. "Alex and Roy, can you look after Lucy, please?"

Alex decided he liked Lucy. He took her hand and helped her over the sand. They were getting along fine until Lucy suddenly sat down. He tried to pull her up again. She made herself limp and very heavy.

"Babies are always trouble," said Roy knowingly.

Next Lucy wrenched off her shoes and threw them away.

"She'll get us into trouble," worried Roy.

"Doos no good," said Lucy.

"She's right," laughed Alex. "Shoes get filled up with sand here." He sat down and took off his shoes. Roy did the same.

"Doos no good," repeated Lucy.

"Clever girl," smiled Alex.

"Don't you lose those shoes," shrieked Alex's mother.

When everything and everybody had arrived at Granny's "good spot", Alex's mother got out her swimming costume. "Bet I'm first in the sea," she said.

"Poof," said Granny. "Lucy and I will be in long before you, won't we, Lucy?" She helped Lucy put on her bright yellow costume, then struggled into hers.

The race was just a trick to get Alex and Roy quickly into their swimming things. They fell for it, of course. They were first down to the water's edge.

The sea looked lovely, gently rolling over the sand. But when you stepped into it, brrr it was cold! Splashes that touched their top halves seemed freezing. Little Lucy shook her head and backed away. Alex's mother shivered. "Time for lunch, I think."

She unpacked all the food and drink and spread out a blanket for the children to sit on. Alex and Roy found it very hard to sit still. They could feel the very digable sand underneath them. Alex accidentally pulled the blanket with his foot. A cup of orange toppled over. It made a little lake on the blanket.

"Sit still," snapped Alex's mother.

"I'm not hungry," wriggled Alex. He got to his feet, causing a shower of sand as he did. "I'm going to build a sandcastle."

"Can I go too?" asked Roy.

"I suppose so," grumbled Alex's mother. "Lug all this food down here and you hardly eat a thing." She looked at Granny. "It's all those ginger snaps they ate in the car."

"Don't worry. They'll be hungry later," consoled Granny.

They packed away the lunch things and then settled back in their chairs, with their eyes shut, to enjoy the hot weather. Lucy played happily beside them. She was picking up handfuls of sand and letting it fall through her fingers.

"Dat's good," said Lucy to herself.

She filled her pockets with sand. "Dat's good," she said again.

She filled Alex's shoes with sand. "Dat's good!"

Alex's mother smiled to herself. It was so sweet listening to little Lucy. It had been no bother bringing her. In the distance she could hear Alex and Roy shouting at each other. She smiled again. They were very good friends, really, in spite of quarrels.

Then she realized Lucy was silent. Very silent. A sign of trouble! Perhaps she'd wandered off . . . got lost? Alex's mother opened her eyes and sat up quickly. It was all right. Lucy was still next to her chair, but, oh, no! She'd emptied everything out of Alex's mother's bag and was filling it with sand.

"No, no, no, no, no," said Alex's mother, taking away the bag and emptying out the sand. "Put back my things," she ordered.

For a moment Lucy looked as if she was going to cry; then she looked up at Alex's mother, saw she meant business, and put the things back.

"Good girl," said Alex's mother.

"Doos," said Lucy, pointing to Alex and Roy's shoes.

"Yes. Shoes," repeated Alex's mother.

"Doos," Lucy pointed wildly at the shoes. "Doos!"

Alex's mother saw sand in Alex's shoes. "Good girl," she thanked Lucy. "Alex would have been cross to find his shoes full of sand." She emptied out the sand.

"Der doos. Der doos," continued Lucy, pointing to Roy's shoes.

"No, they're not full of sand," assured Alex's mother. "Let me see if I can find you a cup or two to fill with sand instead."

Some tall plastic tubs pleased Lucy very much. She played happily all afternoon with them.

Then it was time to go home. Alex's

mother, Granny and Lucy went and admired Alex and Roy's fine sandcastle which was slowly being washed away by the sea.

"We must pack up our things, before they get washed away as well," said Alex's mother.

As before, Alex and Roy's job was to carry the shoes and help Lucy across the sand to the car. When they got there Alex's mother looked worried.

"I can't find the car keys," she said. "They were in my bag. They must have fallen out when I tipped out Lucy's sand."

Everyone groaned and went back to where they'd been sitting. They all searched in the sand for ages. Nothing was found but a few broken shells. Miserably they returned to the car once more.

"I'll go and find a garage," said Alex's mother. "Perhaps they can help. Alex, you can keep me company. Quickly, put your shoes on."

"Can I come too?" asked Roy.

"Yes. Get your shoes on."

Roy put one shoe on then looked up. "There's something in my shoe," he said. "Something lumpy."

It was the keys.

Lucy pointed wildly at the keys. "Der doos, der doos!"

Alex's mother looked puzzled for a moment. What was Lucy on about? Then she smiled. "Lucy! You did it. That's what you were trying to tell me when you put the things back into my bag." She shook her head. "And I didn't listen."

On the way home Alex's mother said nothing. She was tired. The day hadn't gone quite as she'd planned it. A few days afterwards, though, she started telling everybody the story of How Lucy Lost the Keys. It seemed funny then.

8
The Airshow

After days of pleading Alex's mother agreed to take him and Roy to the airshow. They had passed its red and yellow poster with the small somersaulting aeroplane every day on their way to school. Alex had been sure that if he pestered his mother enough she would agree to take them. She had said yes, though she was a bit uncertain about it.

"I've never been to an airshow," she said,

looking worried. "I'm not sure what to expect."

Alex sighed. "Aeroplanes and helicopters, of course!"

He was right; they saw them in the air as they neared the showground. There was a lot more too. Tents, stands, food stalls, bits of machinery, and thousands of people. Alex and Roy were very surprised; it wasn't the sort of airport they'd seen on TV.

They paid their money at the gate and went in. Where to go first was a problem, there was so much to see.

"Let's go to the runway," said Alex. "We can see the planes taking off."

There were signs telling them which way to go. Alex's mother led the way. They stuck close to each other so as not to get lost.

BBBbbrrrroouugggghhh . . . went a plane not far above their heads.

Alex's mother jumped. "Oooh! What a

noise. I didn't realize it would be so noisy at an airshow."

Alex saw some people, including children, getting into a small plane. He tugged at his mother's arm. "Look, they're having a ride. Can we have one? I want a ride. Please!"

Alex's mother had secretly always wanted a ride in a small plane. She'd even thought she would probably get one at this airshow. She hadn't told Alex, not wanting to raise his hopes. But now, when she saw how expensive the rides were, and how long the queue was, she said sadly, "Not today."

BBBrrrrhhrrroouuggggh! screamed another plane overhead.

"Today!" shouted Alex, only half catching what she said.

"No!" bellowed his mother. She was angry and disappointed about the plane ride. She was also fed up with the noise.

The plane flew over again, Bbrrrrrhh-rrouughhh.

"You're mean, Mum," shouted Alex. "I never get anything."

His mother ignored him. "What shall we do next, Roy?" she asked.

"See what's in the big tent?" suggested Roy.

They turned around and walked away from the small plane.

Alex was furious. "Mummm!" he screamed.

She didn't hear. His voice was drowned by another . . .

BBBrrroouuggghhh!

He followed them, kicking the ground.

"Cheer up," said his mother. "There's other things here besides plane rides. Hopefully it'll be quieter away from the runway."

But she was wrong.

EEEEEeeeeeeyyyyyaaaaaAAAhh.

EEEeeeeeeeeyyaaaaaarrrgghh.

Two planes passed low over their heads.

She covered her ears with her hands and looked miserable. Alex and Roy didn't notice the noise. They'd seen lots of stalls giving away stickers with advertisements on them. Alex forgot all about the plane ride. He started collecting stickers, and stuck them all over his T-shirt. Roy did the same. It became a race to see who could get the most.

EEEeeeeeeeeeeyyeerrrr.

Another plane! Alex's mother had had enough.

"Stop a minute," she called. She rummaged in her bag for something to cover her ears with. Alex and Roy hopped up and down. They were impatient to get on.

"Can we go and see if there's stickers in that big tent?" asked Alex.

"Hang on," said his mother. "I'm just looking for something."

BBBrrrroooougghh, rumbled a fast passing plane.

At the same time Alex said, "I won't be a minute," and dashed off.

His mother didn't hear him. When at last she looked up from her bag, smiling, with cotton wool earplugs in, only Roy was there. Her smile faded.

"Where's Alex?" she asked.

"I think he went into that big tent," said Roy.

They went into the tent and looked all around, but they couldn't see Alex.

"Look, Alex's mum," said Roy. "There's a simulator."

"A what?" said Alex's mother, taking out her earplugs.

"You know," said Roy. "You can pretend to be the pilot of a jet. Can I have a go?"

"Later," promised Alex's mother. "We must find Alex."

They looked everywhere for Alex. In all the tents, around the stalls. (Roy collected more stickers.) Down by the planes, even in the toilets. But they didn't find him. Finally, after a few moments' silent thought, Alex's mother said, "There's only one thing to do. Call for him over the public address system."

"The what?" said Roy.

Alex's mother smiled. "You know. The loud voice that announces what's about to happen. Not that it's much good here with all the noisy planes."

Roy liked the idea of having Alex's name called out across the showground, so they went and found the organizers' tent.

The organizers were very busy but kind. They said that as soon as there was a quiet moment they would call for Alex. In the meantime they gave Alex's mother a cup of tea and Roy an orange drink.

Sitting side by side, they waited. Alex's mother pulled out a hanky and dabbed her eyes. Roy saw she was crying.

And Alex? Was he crying?

No. He had walked into the tent next to where his mother had stopped. Just like Roy he had seen the flight simulator. Forgetting all about wanting stickers he went exploring. The enormous pilot's chair was vacant so he sat in it and pretended to fly a jet. It was such a big chair, and Alex was so small, that when his mother and Roy came looking for him, they didn't see him from the back. It wasn't until the man in charge of the simulator told Alex he'd had rather a long go, and ought to let someone else have a turn, that Alex remembered his mother and Roy. He looked round but couldn't see them anywhere.

"Where's my mum?" he asked the man.

"I bet she got tired of waiting for you," said the man. "She's probably gone for a cup of tea. Wait here, I'm sure she'll be back in a minute."

Alex waited and waited.

"I think I'd better take you to the organizers' tent," said the man.

Once inside the organizers' tent Alex saw his mother and Roy, drinks in hand.

Alex was furious. "You left me for a cup of tea! I could have got lost for ever."

"I left you?" shrieked back his mother.

"I've been looking for you all afternoon. You just disappeared."

"I told you where I was going," argued Alex.

"I didn't hear you," grumbled his mother. "Where were you?"

"In the big tent!" said Alex.

"*I* thought he was in that tent," added Roy.

Alex's mother held her breath as if she would burst.

An organizer tried to be cheerful. "Well, have you sorted out yet who lost who?" he laughed.

Alex's mother was furious. "You can laugh, but this is the worst day I've had for ages. I'm never, ever, coming to an airshow again!"

Alex and Roy looked at each other. They'd never seen Alex's mother angry like that before.

The organizer looked down at them all. "Oh, we can't have that. Let me see what I can do. Have you been up for a ride today?" They shook their heads. "Follow me then," said the organizer.

Were they going to get a ride? They followed the organizer through the crowds of people to the runway. There was still a long queue waiting for a ride, but they went straight to the front.

"I have some special guests here," said the organizer. "I'd like them to take the next trip."

Alex and Roy and Alex's mother couldn't believe their luck. Five minutes later they were in the small plane and bumping down the runway. They felt a turn in their stomachs and saw they were rising above the fields and showground. Higher and higher, and around the showground. Tents looked like mushrooms, people a multicoloured mix.

It was even better than they'd imagined.

The time in the air was very short. The plane bumped back down on to the runway. The organizer was still there.

"Will you come again?" he asked.

They all answered, "Yes!"

When they got home Alex's mother put a jar on the sideboard marked "Flying Fund". Alex knew he'd not have to do any pleading to go to the airshow next year. . . Even though the fund soon got emptied for change for his dinner money.

9

The Night Out

When Alex and Roy came home from school one day, they found Alex's mother having a small party in her kitchen.

There was Sue, with baby Lucy asleep on her knee, Roy's mother and Janet from next door. They were very happy, laughing and talking loudly.

"What's going on?" asked Alex.

"Next weekend we're going to have a

night out," said Janet. "All together. It should be fun."

"Can we come too?" asked Alex and Roy.

"No. This is just for grown-ups."

"Why can't we come?" persisted Alex.

"It's in the evening, after you've gone to bed."

Alex pulled himself up straight and tall. "I can stay up late!"

Roy's mother laughed at him. "No! It's your mum's night off. She needs a break from you."

"It's not fair," said Alex. Roy agreed.

Alex's mother sighed, turned her back on them, and went on talking to her friends. She wasn't going to argue.

Alex suddenly remembered he was hungry. "Let's see what's in the fridge," he whispered to Roy.

In the week that followed Alex felt miserable

about his mother having a night out without him. She booked Granny to come and babysit, bought herself a new skirt, and had her hair done.

"What a fuss about going out," grumbled Alex.

"I know," said Roy. "I can't sleep for the sound of the sewing machine. Mum's making herself a new dress."

"It's not fair," they both agreed. "We should have a night out too."

On the morning of the night out, Alex didn't want any breakfast. He stayed in his bedroom sulking. He couldn't stop thinking how unfair his mum was. As it was a Saturday, and not a school day, she left him alone.

At lunchtime she cooked him one of his favourite meals. Alex felt too cross to eat it.

"I hope you're not getting ill," she said. "Do you feel all right?"

"No," Alex moaned. "I feel terrible." His tummy was feeling empty and rumbly. He went and lay on his bed.

A little later Roy came round and asked if he wanted to play.

"Going out in the fresh air might do you good," encouraged Alex's mother. But Alex shook his head.

"No," he said feebly.

"I hope you'll be better by tonight," worried Alex's mother. She felt his forehead.

"You've no fever, but you'd better rest quietly for a while." She tucked him up and gave him a hug.

So Alex stayed in bed. There was nothing to do. Time dragged by very slowly.

Roy's mother came visiting. Alex heard his mother say she might not be able to go on their night out. She didn't want to leave

Alex when he was unwell. Alex smiled to himself.

Then Roy's mother spoke in a quiet voice. Alex tried to hear what she was saying, but he couldn't. It was very annoying.

Suddenly she came into his room. She leaned against his bed.

"What's all this about feeling ill?" she asked. "On our night out! We can't have that. Your mother hasn't had a night out for ages."

"Neither have I," mumbled Alex sadly.

Roy's mother smiled. "Well, why don't you come and spend the night at our house?"

Alex didn't answer.

"Oh, come on," coaxed Roy's mother. "Roy would really like it. Renee'll be there too. I'll make you up a bed in Roy's room."

"All right," said Alex.

Alex's mother cancelled Granny, and from then on Alex made a miraculous recovery. He ate a giant supper that made him feel much better. Then he asked to borrow a suitcase.

He packed his spare clothes, pyjamas, drawing things, games, slippers, rag doll, towel and toothbrush. His mother laughed when she saw Alex sitting on the case trying to get it shut.

"How long are you going for?" she joked.

Alex began to like the idea of going to

Roy's house more and more. He didn't have to go to bed when it was his bedtime, because his mother wasn't going out till late.

"It's not worth you going to bed and then getting up again," she explained.

Long after it was dark they walked round to Roy's house.

Roy was still up. He was watching a film on TV.

"This is really good," he said, without even looking up.

Alex sat down and watched the film too. He hardly noticed his mother kiss him goodnight and leave with her friends.

When the film ended, Renee quickly turned off the TV.

"Off to bed now, you boys," she said.

They blinked and slowly stood up.

"Quickly!" shouted Renee. "It's late!"

Alex heaved his suitcase up to Roy's room.

"What you got in there?" enquired Roy.

"I'll show you," said Alex, flinging back the lid.

"Wow!" said Roy. "Are you staying for ever?"

"Are you in bed yet?" called up Renee. "I'll give you five minutes. Then the light goes off."

Roy giggled. "Let's get into bed. We can get up again when she's gone."

So they did, with all their clothes on! They lay flat on their backs, covers pulled up to their chins, arms straight by their sides.

They waited and waited, but Renee didn't come. The doorbell rang, some people came in, and some music was turned on very loud.

"Are you still awake?" hissed Roy.

"Yes," whispered Alex. "What's going on downstairs?"

"Renee's friends," said Roy. "Shall we take a look?"

Alex and Roy carefully got out of bed, and crept down the stairs. Luckily the light was still on. The living room door was not quite shut. They pushed it open until they could see Renee and her friends. They were sitting on the carpet talking.

It was interesting at first to watch and not be seen, but then it got boring.

"I'm hungry," said Alex.

"Mum made some coconut cakes today," remembered Roy. "They're in the kitchen. Shall I try and sneak across the living room and get them?"

Alex liked the idea. They looked to see how it could be done without being seen by Renee and her friends. It looked quite easy. They were at the other side of the room.

Bending low, so he was hidden by a settee, Roy dashed across to the kitchen. A few minutes later he dashed back with a tin.

The coconut cakes were very good. They ate them all. Then Alex was thirsty!

"You're hopeless," groaned Roy. "I suppose I'll have to do it again." He dashed to the kitchen once more.

Time went by and Roy didn't return. Alex began to worry. Then Renee stood up. She walked towards the kitchen.

Oh, no, thought Alex. She'll see him.

He was right. "Aaah!" shrieked Renee. "Roy! What are you doing here?"

Alex didn't wait to hear more. He ran back up the stairs, jumped into bed and pulled the covers up to his chin again.

Roy soon came up. He was carrying two drinks. He was laughing. "I told her the music woke us up. She was very sorry."

They sat in their beds and drank their drinks.

"I wonder what my mum's doing now," said Alex.

"Dancing?" suggested Roy.

"Like this?" giggled Alex, jumping out of bed and prancing up and down to the sound of Renee's music.

"Noooo," laughed Roy. "You look like a robot. You've got to sway a little."

"Round like this?"

Alex swung his arms around himself like a human helicopter. There was a loud crashing sound and a great stack of tapes fell to the floor.

"Idiot!" hissed Roy.

"What are you up to?" asked Renee's voice.

Alex and Roy slid down into their beds and shut their eyes shut.

"I know you're not asleep," said Renee. "I heard you."

Alex and Roy tried to hold themselves perfectly still.

"Come on. What have you been up to?"

Alex wanted to giggle so much he began to shake. Then he heard voices.

His mother was saying, "I haven't enjoyed myself so much for years."

And Roy's mother was saying, "Phew, I'm exhausted. It was a good evening. Where's Renee?"

"I'm in Roy's bedroom," she called down.

"Are they all right?" Alex's mother sounded worried.

"Yes," said Renee. "I thought they were still awake, but now I look, they seem fast asleep again."

Unseen by Alex she beckoned his mother upstairs.

"If Alex had still been awake," said his mother, "he could have come home with me."

There was silence. Alex opened one eye to see if his mother was still there. She was staring down at him.

"Coming home?" she asked. Alex nodded. It would be easy. He still had his clothes on.

Roy's father saw them home. He carried Alex's suitcase.

"I had a lovely time," said Alex's mother. "How about you, Alex?"

"Really good," said Alex. "I'll go again when you want another night out." He gave a yawn. "But can I always come home to sleep?"

10
Granny's Accident

Alex's granny didn't live far from Alex and his mother. News of her accident reached them very quickly. Roy's mother rushed around all hot and out of breath.

"Your granny's had a fall. She was standing on a stool, in her garden, cleaning the windows, when it tipped up. She's in terrible pain. It's her leg. We've sent for an ambulance."

By the time Alex and his mother got round to Granny's house the ambulance had already been. It had taken her off to the local hospital. Alex's mother looked a little stunned.

"Jump in my car," said Roy's father. "I'll take you to the hospital."

Alex hadn't said anything since they had heard the news. He felt frightened. He hoped nothing bad had happened to his granny. His mother noticed his worried face.

"You all right, Alex?" she enquired.

"Will Granny get better?" Alex asked.

"Of course," reassured his mother. "At the worst, if her leg is broken, they'll put it in a plaster cast, and she may have to stay in hospital for a week or two."

At the thought of a plaster cast Alex cheered up. "A boy at school had one of those. Big and white it was, all over his arm. We drew on it. Can I draw on Granny's?"

Alex's mother gave a little laugh and hugged Alex. "You do cheer me up," she said. "We must remember we don't know for sure yet if Granny has broken her leg."

Roy's father dropped them off outside the hospital. "I'll wait for you in the car park," he said.

"You'll find your granny in the third door," said the receptionist.

Alex ran ahead. One, two, three. He opened the door and looked for his granny. He was expecting to see her in bed, her leg in white plaster. But she was sitting on a chair, her foot on a low stool, a small white bandage around her ankle.

Alex was disappointed. "She hasn't broken her leg," he said crossly.

His mother would have told him off if she had heard what he said. Luckily for Alex she was too busy asking Granny how she felt.

"It's very painful," groaned Granny.

"She can go home now," said a nurse. "We've X-rayed her ankle and it's only sprained."

Granny looked shocked. "I can't walk. I know I can't walk."

"It's not as bad as you think," said the nurse. "I'll give you a walking stick. You'll be getting about as normal in a couple of days."

"Stick!" said Granny grumpily. "Sticks are

for old ladies. You won't catch me using one."

Alex's mother took the stick and thanked the nurse. She helped Granny stand up. She put her arm around her. Alex did the same on the other side. Together they almost carried her to the car park. They had to carry her again when they reached her house.

"I'm sorry to cause all this bother," sniffed Granny. "Standing on that stool was a very silly thing to do."

"Don't worry, we'll look after you," smiled Alex's mother. "Won't we, Alex?"

Every day after that Alex's mother cooked some extra dinner and took it round to Granny on a tray. Even though she lived very near, by the end of the week Alex's mother was becoming tired of looking after Granny.

"I wouldn't mind," she explained. "But I'm sure her ankle is better now. She won't even try and use her stick. It's so silly. She's getting all sad and cross stuck indoors. Tomorrow, Alex, I think you could carry round her dinner. You could ask if there's any jobs she needs doing. Take Roy with you. He's good at helping."

Alex liked the idea. His granny was good fun, and she always had delicious things in her cupboard; often surprises too.

He gobbled down his lunch, and then walked round to Roy's carrying the tray. He

would have liked to run; but the dinner on the tray rattled too much.

Roy carried the tray on to Granny's.

Alex had her front door key; so he rang the bell and then opened the door.

"What a nice surprise to see you," said Granny. "I haven't seen anybody all week."

"Here's your dinner," said Alex. "Are there any jobs we can do?"

"Well," began Granny. "You can post some letters. I've written such a lot since I've been trapped in this house."

It was an easy job. The post box was right outside the house. There were six letters. They posted three each.

"What's the next job?" asked Alex.

"I've lost my glasses," Granny said sadly. "This bad leg is making me so forgetful. Could you find them?"

They hunted and hunted. Then Granny found them down her chair!

"Any more jobs?" asked Roy.

Granny thought and thought. "I know! You can sweep the leaves off my garden path. I can see them through the window. It looks such a mess."

So Alex and Roy started sweeping. It was the time of year when leaves are yellow and brown and fall from trees. As fast as they swept them up, new ones fell.

"I don't like this job," said Alex, throwing down his broom. "I'm going to ask Granny for a cake and a drink."

Granny shook her head. "Sorry, I've nothing left. I can't get to the shops with this bad leg of mine." Then suddenly she brightened. "You could go to the super-market for me!"

Alex and Roy weren't sure. The super-market was a long way up the road; they didn't usually go on their own. But it would be an adventure. They agreed to go.

Granny wrote them out a shopping list, and before they left she checked that they could read it. It was a good thing she did!

"Tie," read Roy.

"Tea," corrected Granny.

"Cack," said Alex.

"Cake," said Granny.

"Bread," read Roy.

"Good," congratulated Granny.

"Ch . . . Ch . . . Chess," stuttered Alex.

"Cheese," corrected Granny.

"Seats?" puzzled Roy with a giggle.

"Sweets," said Granny. "For you two. For being so helpful."

Roy carefully folded the list and put it in his pocket. They took a shopping bag each and set off feeling very important.

Alex often went shopping with his mother so he knew what to do. Before entering the supermarket he picked up a wire basket. Roy did the same. They got out the list and began searching for the things. It was like a treasure hunt.

Alex found the tea, and put it in his basket.

Roy found the cheese, and put it in his basket.

Alex found the bread, Roy the cake.

They chose their own sweets.

Then they queued at the checkout. They felt very pleased with themselves.

"Are you two together?" asked the cashier.

Alex and Roy nodded.

She tapped up their shopping on her till. "Three forty-three," she said, holding out her hand.

Alex didn't understand. Roy was loading his shopping into his bag, so Alex did the same.

"Three forty-three," demanded the cashier. She sounded cross now. Alex and

Roy didn't know what to do. She noticed their blank faces and changed her tone. "Money," she said. "I need money for the things you've bought."

Alex was shocked. He didn't have any money. He looked at Roy. He didn't have any money either. Granny had forgotten to give them any.

"The shopping's for my granny," explained Alex. "She's got a bad leg."

The cashier nodded. "I'll keep the shopping here, while one of you runs home to get the money."

"I'll go," said Roy.

"I'm not staying on my own," complained Alex.

"I'm not either," said Roy. He started to leave. Alex grabbed his arm.

"I'm going. It's my granny!"

Suddenly they heard a loud tapping noise. They stopped. They saw Alex's granny banging on the shop window with her new walking stick. She was waving her purse.

She hobbled into the shop and paid the cashier.

When she spoke to Alex and Roy she was smiling. "It was a good thing you forgot the money, or I would never have dared try to walk. And you know, my leg doesn't hurt half as much as I thought it would. I think this calls for a little celebration. What about a fizzy drink or something in the coffee shop?"

Alex and Roy thought it sounded a very good idea. They were tired and hungry from being so helpful, and Alex had something extra to celebrate . . . His granny was her old kind, smiley self again.

11
The Patchwork Toboggan

Alex woke in a chilly bedroom. Outside was strangely bright. There was a little line of white along the bottom of the window. It took a few moments for Alex to think, then he sprang from his bed. "Snow!" he shrieked.

In a desperate rush he dragged on his trousers and shuffled into his shoes. He would have gone out like that, with his pyjama top still on, if his mother hadn't grabbed him. "It's very cold out there. You must dress up warmly."

Alex quickly added a jumper and escaped from the flat. "You'll be cold," shouted his mother, but Alex was too excited to stop.

The grass in front of the flats was now a big white rectangle. It was early, so it was untouched except for a few dog footprints. Alex walked straight across the middle. His was the first human trail.

He tried to make a snowball, but the snow was too crumbly. His mother came out in her woolly coat. She looked like a teddy bear.

"I'm off down to the shops," she said. "Got to take the washing to the launderette and do some shopping. Coming?"

"Are you going in the car?" Alex asked.

"Yes, if it'll start."

They walked over to the road and found the car completely covered with snow. It had a row of icicles like teeth across the front.

Alex thought it looked like a snow dinosaur. He didn't want to scrape off all the snow, but his mother insisted. "I *must* get to the shops."

So they cleared it. Then Alex's mother got in and tried to start the engine. She turned the key again and again. There were short wheezing noises, then nothing. She got out and scratched her head. "It's not going to go," she said sadly.

"I'm cold," said Alex. "I'm going in."

"Good idea," agreed his mother. "I can think better in the warm."

So they went in, had warm drinks, and thought about the snow.

"I do like snow," pondered Alex.

"I half like it," said his mother. "It's good to play with, but mostly it means trouble."

"Yes, you can play lots of games," agreed Alex. "You can make snowballs and snowmen, slide on the ice, and toboggan in the park." Alex stopped. He remembered something. "Hey, Mum, last year you promised that this year you'd make a toboggan. Can you do it now? Please. Please!"

"No. Not now. I'm busy. I've somehow got to . . ." began Alex's mother, but her words faded away. Suddenly she grinned broadly and flung her arms around Alex. "You're brilliant, Alex! Brilliant."

Alex sat opened-mouthed in surprise. What was she on about?

"If we made a toboggan," she explained, "we could carry the washing and shopping on it. That's what people did before they had cars. And afterwards you could have it to play with."

Alex thought it was a wonderful idea.

"To work then," said his mother.

There was the little problem of what to make it with. There were very few pieces of wood left in the cupboard. Alex had the idea of using his wooden car box. He didn't mind having a cardboard one instead.

"That makes it easy," smiled his mother.

They made it in half an hour, complete with a rope handle. Alex's mother called it their patchwork toboggan, because it was made from odd pieces of wood.

"It really needs some metal strips underneath," she said. "But it'll do just for today. We'd better get going," she added. "Looks like it might snow again."

So Alex carefully carried the new toboggan down their steps. His mother followed with the bag of washing. Once on level ground they loaded it on. Then Alex pulled the rope. He was surprised how easily the toboggan slipped behind him.

On the road they met Roy's father trying to start his car.

"What's that thing?" he laughed.

"Our toboggan," said Alex proudly.

"Toboggan?" teased Roy's father. "Looks like a heap of old firewood."

"Bet we get to the shops before you," said

Alex's mother. She noted the familiar row of icicle teeth along the front of the car.

They hurried on. Alex wanted his mother to pull him along with the washing.

"A great lump like you," she shrieked. "You must be joking."

Disappointed, Alex walked slowly, dragging his boots through the snow.

His mother took the route through the park to the shops. She stopped at the top of the hill.

"Hurry up, Alex," she called. "We can both have a ride down this bit."

Alex's mother sat at the front, then Alex. He was sandwiched between her and the washing.

"Now we'll see if it works," said Alex's mother, giving a big kick backwards.

They sped off down the hill very fast.

"Help!" cried Alex's mother. "I can't

steer. Hold tight, Alex. I think we're going to hit that bump."

They did. Sssshmack! Alex, his mother and all the washing were flung off sideways.

They were shaken but not hurt. Washing was scattered everywhere. "Thank goodness we weren't in the car," said Alex's mother.

They picked up the socks and pants, T-shirts, trousers and other washing and put it back in the bag, put the bag back on the toboggan and continued on their way.

Their first stop was the launderette, then the supermarket. Both places Alex insisted on staying outside to guard the toboggan. When they returned to the launderette the assistant there invited Alex and his toboggan to come inside. Alex was pleased; he was beginning to feel cold and wet.

It was hot and steamy inside the launderette, which made it feel very cold outside when it was time to return home.

The toboggan felt very heavy. It carried shopping as well as washing now.

They went the road way home. "I can't face that hill in the park," said Alex's mother.

It began to snow so heavily it was difficult to see where they were going.

"Cor!" said Alex. "It's just like going to the North Pole. I've seen pictures of explorers. They have dogs to pull their toboggans. Next year, if Roy gets his dog, we can use it to pull the toboggan."

But there was to be no next year for the toboggan. As Alex spoke it stopped. It had broken. The runners had splayed outwards and the seat with the washing and shopping on had fallen in!

"Can you mend it?" Alex asked.

"No," replied his mother. "It's had it! We'll have to carry the things home. I can manage the shopping and washing if you can bring the toboggan."

Alex felt very sad. He looked lovingly at the toboggan. "Stupid thing. Why did it break?" he cried.

"It was only a patchwork toboggan," explained his mother. "We did make it very quickly, and it wasn't so stupid. It carried the washing all the way to the launderette, and nearly all the way back. Look over there. There's Roy and his dad still trying to start their car."

Alex's face brightened. "We beat you! We beat you!" he shouted.

Roy's father pulled a long face. "You did. But what has happened to your toboggan?"

"It broke," said Alex.

Roy's father nodded knowingly.

"It nearly lasted," said Alex's mother. "I got all my washing and shopping done."

"Very good," congratulated Roy's father.

"Tell you what. I've some wood and metal strips at home just right for making a toboggan. Would you like them?"

Alex and his mother nodded eagerly.

After lunch they went and collected the wood and metal strips. On the way Alex dumped the patchwork toboggan in the dustbin. He didn't feel sad. They were about to make an extra special toboggan, very carefully this time. It had a plan, measurements, expensive brass screws that wouldn't go rusty, and metal runners.

Like everything it took much longer than expected to make. Two whole days! Alex worried that the snow would melt before they were finished. But it didn't. In fact, Alex couldn't go out when it was ready because it was snowing too hard. He had to wait till the next day to show Roy.

Proudly he dragged the toboggan round to Roy's house and rang the doorbell.

Bernice peeped through the curtains. "It's Alex!" she screamed. Immediately all Roy's family were on the doorstep admiring the toboggan. All, that is, except Bernice. She was busily putting on her boots, scarf, coat, hat and mittens, all ready for a ride.

"You'll have to give her one," laughed Roy's mother.

Alex didn't mind, he wanted to show off his new toboggan. He liked Bernice, and she wasn't half as heavy as the washing and shopping had been.

12
The Robot

Alex's mother was tired. She sat at the kitchen table stirring her coffee round and round. Her face was pale and long.

Poor Mum, thought Alex. "What's the matter?" he asked.

"Oh, I'm just tired," she said. "There's so much to do: things in the flat, the car, looking after you and Granny."

"What you need to make your life easier,"

said Alex very seriously, "is a robot. I'll make one for you."

"That's a lovely idea," smiled his mother. "What are you going to make it out of?"

"This and that," said Alex casually. He really hadn't a clue! "I'll see what I can find." He started to hunt for thises and thats.

To begin with the robot needed a body. Alex couldn't find one anywhere. Then he noticed his car box, a large square cardboard box; that would do. He tipped out all the cars.

"Wait a minute!" cried his mother. "That's not helping, that's making more mess."

"I'll clear it up later," promised Alex.

Next the head. It needed something like a bucket. Alex found a yellow one under the sink. There were a few sticky cartons inside; he took them out.

"Hey, Alex," called his mother. "Where are you taking my rubbish bin?"

"It's just what I need for my robot's head."

"No," said his mother firmly. "Put it back. And what was in it. I'll find you something else."

A large plastic bottle was as near as she could get.

"Okay," said Alex. "I'll cut the top off, then it will look more like a head."

But could he get it straight? No. He trimmed more and more off the bottle, till it was the size of a small flower pot. It left a great heap of trimmings on the floor.

His mother frowned and pointed to the trimmings.

"I'll clear it up later," promised Alex. He was already puzzling over how to fix the head to the body. It could be tricky. He tried glue. That didn't work at all. It stuck to his fingers and made a sticky patch on the floor which he hoped his mother wouldn't notice.

He tried nailing the head and body together. He used a hammer and nails from his mother's toolbox. But even with a piece of wood behind it didn't work; the plastic was too bendy.

Alex's mother stared at the open toolbox.

"I'm clearing up later," repeated Alex.

Then he tried string, and that didn't work. There was nothing to tie it to.

Alex felt like giving up. "Stupid thing," he said, dumping it on the ground.

"Oh, you can't give up now," said his mother. "I need a helper more than ever now, with all the mess you've made. I wonder if we could sew it together?"

She opened up her sewing box and after a little raking found an enormous needle, the one she used to mend holes in the chair covers and sew handles back on to bags.

"This should do," she said, threading it with some thick black cotton.

The head sewed on easily, but it looked a bit silly, such a little head on a big box body. Alex's mother thought a hat would help. She sewed on a woolly bobble hat. "It's still not quite right," she pondered. "Perhaps a face would help." Alex drew one on with his thick felt-tip pens, but still it didn't look like a robot.

Alex and his mother screwed up their faces in thought.

"Arms and legs!" shouted Alex. "He needs arms and legs."

"Cardboard tubes?" suggested his mother.

A good idea but there were none in the flat.

"Perhaps Granny or Roy will have some," suggested Alex's mother.

Alex went to see.

Roy was pleased when Alex arrived. He was feeling rather lonely. Everybody in his house was too busy to play with him. He found a lot of tubes for the robot, but Alex still wanted to go on and get some more from his granny.

"I want to see this robot," nagged Roy.

"Later," said Alex. "We need lots and lots of tubes. I'm sure Granny'll have some. She keeps everything. She was very poor once."

Alex's granny had a whole bag of cardboard tubes.

"Told you," said Alex to Roy. "Thank you, Granny."

"Don't go yet," insisted Granny. "I'll see if I've got anything else for you."

Alex grinned at Roy. "Bet she has," he whispered.

She came back smiling. "Here's a bar each. You do like chocolate, don't you, Roy?"

"Yes, thank you," said Roy.

They returned to Alex's, their tube hunt successful.

"I think sewing would be best again for joining on these tubes," said Alex's mother.

Alex and Roy tried sewing, but the needles dug into their fingers. "Oooh! Ouch! Aaah!" they went.

"Give it here," said Alex's mother. "I can't bear to hear you suffer so."

She joined together four lots of tubes, and attached them to four corners of the box body. Now the robot had long swingy arms and legs. She held him up by the bobble on his hat. He was as tall as her. Alex and Roy clapped with delight. "But does it work?" enquired Alex's mother.

"Of course," said Alex.

"Can it really clean up?" she teased.

"Yes," said Alex. "I'll show you."

The robot did get all the mess cleared away, but it looked as if Roy was doing all the work. The robot's body acted as a rubbish bin. Alex held it straight as he followed after Roy, who found bits to go in it.

When all was tidy Alex's mother thought it was time for a little snack. She found she had a problem. With the robot sitting at the table there was no room for her. She had to stand.

Later, when she wanted to sit in her comfy chair and watch TV, the robot was there. Alex said she mustn't move him, he'd had a busy day tidying up. She had to sit on the floor.

At bedtime, Alex wanted to take the robot to bed with him, but he didn't fit.

"Could you have him in your bed?" Alex asked his mother. "He's very tired."

Alex's mother looked at Alex in amazement. "Tired! I'm the one that's tired! Robots never get tired, and anyway, they sleep standing up. There's a nail over the kitchen door that you used to swing from when you were a baby. I'll tie him up to that."

She did.

Alex woke early the next morning. He peeped round his bedroom door to see if the robot was still there. At first glance it looked very scary, like a real person, a large person, almost a giant. But when he looked properly, saw the arms and legs, the very long thin tube arms and legs, he smiled; there was his robot.

It scared Granny though.

She saw its shadow through the frosty glass of the front door. "Are you all right?" she asked in a worried voice when Alex opened the door. "Who's that giant person in the kitchen?"

When Alex showed her his robot she laughed. "I thought it was real."

For several days the robot stayed hanging in the kitchen doorway. He wasn't much good at housework, but he made a good watchman. He scared away unwanted visitors, and frightened Alex and his mother when they bumped into him in the dark.

The only person not to be scared was Roy. Perhaps because he always peeped through the letter box after ringing the bell. Perhaps because Alex had boasted that robots were better guards than dogs, and Roy was very fond of dogs. Whatever the reason, whenever Roy spoke about Alex's robot he called it "a load of old toilet rolls".

13
The Terrible Day

It's funny how some days everything goes wrong. Poor Roy had one of those days.

His mother had promised to take him out to buy some new clothes. Bernice was in one of her crying moods, and then his mother noticed she had spots, possibly chicken pox, so they had to stay at home.

Alex came round all happy and bouncy.

His mother had booked them a holiday by the sea.

"Huh!" grunted Roy. "You get all the luck. I can't even go down to the shops 'cos Bernice has got the chicken pox. It's not fair."

"You could play outside," said his mother. "Bernice might sleep if it's quiet in here."

"I came on my bike," said Alex. "We could ride together around the block."

For a moment Roy cheered up, then he found the chain had come off his bike. It wouldn't go back on.

His face screwed up and he crumpled to the floor.

"It's not fair," he said, thumping the floor. "Stupid Bernice. Stupid bike!"

Alex looked kindly at his friend. "It's all right," he said gently. "We can take turns on my bike if you like."

Roy cheered up again. They went out riding.

Alex let Roy have the first turn. He found himself a box to sit on while he waited.

Suddenly from inside the box came a faint meow. Alex sat still and listened. There was a scratching noise, and then, to Alex's horror, a scraggy creature pulled itself from a hole near his legs. He jumped away. From a safe distance he looked again. It was a kitten. A kitten in a terrible state. Its eyes were only half open. They seemed glued shut. Its fur was lumpy and greasy and clung to its very thin body. It moved closer to Alex. He shrank back. He liked kittens but he'd never seen one like this before.

Roy came back and said, "Your turn now," but Alex didn't hear.

The kitten wanted to rub itself against Alex's leg. He moved away. He felt a little sorry for the kitten but he didn't want it mucking up his trousers.

Roy began to shout. "If you don't want your turn I'll . . ." when he noticed that Alex was watching something.

"What's that?" he asked.

"A kitten," said Alex. "Come and look."

Roy laid down the bike and came over.

"Ugh!" he shuddered. "It's all manky."

The kitten stepped over to Roy. It tried to rub itself against *his* leg now. Roy jumped away. "Shoo! Shooo! You're a dirty kitten."

The kitten seemed to like Roy. It tried again. Roy moved. The kitten followed.

"You're too dirty," said Roy. "I don't want you."

He moved backwards. The kitten continued to follow him.

"Hey, Alex!" shouted Roy. "Do something. That manky kitten's after me."

Alex just laughed.

"Shoo, go away!" screamed Roy, running backwards.

Alex laughed so much he nearly fell over. Then he saw Roy's mother coming. He could see what was going to happen; but he was laughing so much he couldn't get the words out to warn Roy.

"Go away, kitten," shrieked Roy, still running backwards. "You need a bath."

There was a soft bumff, and Roy crashed into his mother. He jumped slightly into the air. "Oh, Mum, you frightened me," he said crossly.

"Why ever were you running backwards?" enquired his mother.

"It's that kitten," complained Roy.

"What kitten?" asked his mother. "I can't see any kitten."

"It's there," smiled Alex, pointing to where the kitten was rubbing itself over Roy's shoe.

Roy froze with horror. "Ugh! Get it off!" he screamed.

"Oooh. Poor thing," cooed Roy's mother. "Looks as if it has fallen in some oil. We must take it home and wash it, right away."

Alex and Roy thought that was a good idea, but they began to argue over who was going to carry it back.

"I'm not touching it," said Roy.

Alex shuddered at the thought. "It's Roy's friend, not mine."

"What a pair of babies!" laughed Roy's mother. She picked up the kitten, and holding it at arm's length, led the way home. "Don't leave that bike out," she reminded the boys.

Alex and Roy looked at each other. "It's your turn," they both said together.

"What funny friends you are," sighed Roy's mother. "Well, whichever one of you isn't getting the bike, could you please hold this kitten while I get my key out."

That decided it. In a flash Alex started

back to pick up the bike. "It's your kitten, remember," he shouted to Roy.

Roy looked unhappy again. Carefully he took the kitten from his mother and followed her indoors.

"Shhh," said his mother. "Bernice has gone to sleep. We'll wash the kitten in the kitchen."

Roy put the kitten down next to the sink. It was shaking with fright. "We'll soon have you clean," he told it gently.

Roy's mother filled a basin with soapy water, and Roy held the kitten by the scruff

of its neck while she washed it. It didn't like the water. It hissed and spat and tried to wriggle away backwards. Roy felt frightened, but he kept holding on. He wished Alex was there to help. Alex had gone to talk to Bernice, who had just woken up.

When they thought the kitten must be clean, they wrapped it in a towel and rubbed it dry in front of the heater. Its fur was all fluffy now.

"We must clean its eyes," said Roy's mother, and she fetched a small bowl of water and some cotton wool. With sideways strokes she wiped its eyes until they were clean and open. Big yellow and black eyes!

"See if it'll play with you," suggested Roy's mother.

He tapped the kitten's paw. The kitten tapped Roy's hand. Its tail swished playfully from side to side.

"It *is* playing!" Roy shouted happily.

"Can we have a go?" said Alex, helping a very spotty Bernice unravel herself from some blankets on the settee.

"It's mine," said Roy. "I made it better. You wouldn't help." He scooped the kitten up on to his knee.

"I found it," said Alex. "Let's have a go." He and Bernice crowded round Roy.

"No," said Roy, clasping the kitten tightly to his chest.

The kitten didn't like this. It wriggled and writhed its way out of his arms and jumped down on to the floor. Both Alex and Bernice made a dive for it. Somehow, someone knocked over the little bowl of water they'd used to clean the kitten's eyes. It went all over Roy's trousers.

"I'm wet!" he cried miserably. "It's all your fault. I hate you both. Go away! Go away!" He was screaming now.

Roy's mother tried to calm things down.

"Take those wet trousers off and put them on the heater. They'll be dry in no time. You've got another pair in your drawer."

Roy got to his feet. He picked up the kitten, and folded his arms lovingly around it. "You're my friend," he told it. He gave an angry look to Alex and Bernice. "They're not my friends." He took the kitten with him to his bedroom.

Roy's mother looked at Alex and raised

her eyebrows. "It seems as if that kitten's here to stay."

Alex folded his arms across his chest. Why should Roy get the kitten and not him? he thought crossly.

"Mum! Mum!" called Roy from his bed-room. His voice sounded tiny. "Come here."

"What's the matter now?" sighed his mother. She went to see.

"Oh, no!" Alex heard her say.

She came back. She looked very fed up. "He's got the chicken pox now. Got a fever too. I wondered what was up with him; he's been in a funny mood all day. Sorry, Alex, but you'll have to go home."

Alex went and said goodbye to Roy. He was lying rather sadly in his bed. He pointed to the kitten. It was asleep in front of his heater. "It likes it here," said Roy.

Alex nodded and smiled. "That's good. I've been thinking. I couldn't have had it

anyway. My cats don't like sharing their things with strangers."

Roy smiled back. "It's instead of a dog. Okay?"

"Okay," agreed Alex.

He and Roy were friends again.

Alex wheeled his bike home. He didn't want to ride it. He wanted to have a good long think on the way. Roy's mother had said it would be at least a week before Roy could play again. Alex didn't mind. Sometimes he liked just being by himself.

YOUng HiPPO SPOOKY

Do you like to be spooked? Do you dare to be
scared? If you're *really* brave, then get stuck into
these deliciously spooky but funny ghost stories
from Young Hippo Spooky!

Scarem's House
Malcolm Yorke

When the ghostly house belonging to Scarem
O'Gool and his family is invaded by humans,
there's only one solution. The O'Gools are going to
have to *haunt* them out!

The Screaming Demon Ghostie
Jean Chapman

A Young Hippo Spooky story for early readers

Kate Kelly doesn't believe there's any such thing as
the Screaming Demon Ghostie of the old forest
track. And one dark night, she sets off to prove it!

YOUNG HIPPO MAGIC

Magic is in the air with these enchanting stories from Young Hippo Magic – stories about ordinary, everyday children who discover that in the world of magic, anything is possible!

The Little Pet Dragon
Philippa Gregory

James is thrilled when he finds a tiny greyhound puppy! But aren't those scales on its body? And isn't that snouty face rather dragon-like? James doesn't notice, because his puppy is glimmering with a very strong magic . . .

My Friend's a Gris-Quok
Malorie Blackman

A Young Hippo Magic story for early readers

Alex has a deep, dark secret. He's half Gris-Quok, which is fantastic, because he can turn himself into anything he likes! However, he can only do it *three* times a day . . .

The Marmalade Pony
Linda Newbery

A Young Hippo Magic story for early readers

Hannah has always longed for a pony of her very own, but the best she can do is imagine. Then one day her dad starts making something mysterious in the shed . . .

BABYSITTERS LITTLE SISTER

Meet Karen Brewer. She's seven years old and her big sister Kristy runs the Babysitters Club. And Karen's always having adventures of her own . . . Read all about her in her very own series.

No 1: **Karen's Witch**
No 2: **Karen's Roller Skates**
No 3: **Karen's Worst Day**
No 4: **Karen's Kittycat Club**
No 5: **Karen's School Picture**
No 6: **Karen's Little Sister**
No 7: **Karen's Birthday**
No 8: **Karen's Haircut**
No 9: **Karen's Sleepover**
No 10: **Karen's Grandmothers**
No 11: **Karen's Prize**
No 12: **Karen's Ghost**
No 13: **Karen's Surprise**
No 14: **Karen's New Year**
No 15: **Karen's in Love**
No 16: **Karen's Goldfish**
No 17: **Karen's Brothers**
No 18: **Karen's Home Run**
No 19: **Karen's Goodbye**
No 20: **Karen's Carnival**
No 21: **Karen's New Teacher**

Look out for:

No 22: **Karen's Little Witch**
No 23: **Karen's Doll**
No 24: **Karen's School Trip**
No 25: **Karen's Pen Pal**
No 26: **Karen's Ducklings**

*If you like animals, then you'll love
Hippo Animal Stories!*

Look out for:

Animal Rescue by Bette Paul

Tessa finds life in the country *so* different from life in the town. Will she ever be accepted? But everything changes when she meets Nora and Ned who run the village animal sanctuary, and becomes involved in a struggle to save the badgers of Delves Wood from destruction . . .

Thunderfoot by Deborah van der Beek

Mel Whitby has always loved horses, and when she comes across an enormous but neglected horse in a railway field, she desperately wants to take care of it. But little does she know that taking care of Thunderfoot will change her life forever . . .

A Foxcub Named Freedom
by Brenda Jobling

A vixen lies seriously injured in the undergrowth. Her young son comes to her for comfort and warmth. The cub wants to help his mother to safety, but it is impossible. The vixen, sensing danger, nudges him away, caring nothing for herself – only for his freedom . . .